★ *For Lily John, who showed me her fairy letters,*
and for Josie, just because ★ *A.D.*

★ *For Helena, Denise and Julie,*
thank you all ★ *V.C.*

First published 2003 by Walker Books Ltd
87 Vauxhall Walk, London SE11 5HJ

This edition produced 2003 for The Book People Ltd,
Hall Wood Avenue, Haydock, St Helens WA11 9UL

10 9 8 7 6 5 4 3 2

Text © 2003 Alan Durant
Illustrations © 2003 Vanessa Cabban

The right of Alan Durant and Vanessa Cabban to be identified as author and illustrator respectively
of this work has been asserted by them in accordance with the Copyright, Designs and Patents Act 1988

This book has been typeset in Palatino   Printed in China

British Library Cataloguing in Publication Data:
a catalogue record for this book is available
from the British Library

ISBN 0-7445-8858-8

Dear Tooth Fairy

Alan Durant

illustrated by

Vanessa Cabban

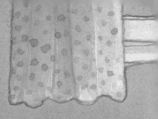

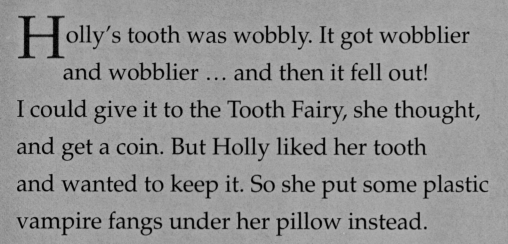

Holly's tooth was wobbly. It got wobblier and wobblier … and then it fell out! I could give it to the Tooth Fairy, she thought, and get a coin. But Holly liked her tooth and wanted to keep it. So she put some plastic vampire fangs under her pillow instead.

"The Tooth Fairy should be happy, because she's getting *lots* of teeth," she said to herself. Next morning the vampire fangs were still there. But there was a tiny envelope too.

HOLLY

Holly read the note from the Tooth Fairy over and over. She was so pleased. I must write back, she thought. This is what she wrote:

Dear Tooth Fairy,

Thank you for coming last night! I've never had a visit from a tooth fairy before. Could you answer some questions please?

What do you want my tooth for?

How did you know it had come out?

Are there Lots of tooth fairies or are you the only one?

Where do you live?

Please answer.

Love Holly

P.S. I drew a picture of you.

I hope you like it.

Holly put the letter under her pillow.

That night the Tooth Fairy came back.

When Holly looked under her pillow
next morning, her note had gone.
In its place was a new envelope.

HOLLY

Holly read the letter and looked
at the leaflet. She thought
about all the tooth fairies,
flying hither and thither through
the starry sky.

All that day Holly wondered about
Fairyland and what it must be like.
She wrote another note
to the Tooth Fairy.

Dear Tooth Fairy,
Thank you so much for your letter.
I'm glad you liked my picture, but
(please don't be cross!!!) there's
just one more thing I need to know
(well, two things actually).
Are there lots of different sorts of fairy?
And what do they do all day and night?
If the fairies want my tooth, I need to know
that they will be good owners, don't I?

Love,
Holly

Holly read the letter and studied her poster. She liked it very much. She wanted to help the Tooth Fairy but she still wasn't sure about giving up her tooth. Then she had an idea.

Dear Tooth Fairy,
Thank you for the poster! It's beautiful!
   I think all the fairies are lovely, but I like tooth fairies the best!
   Do you like riddles? I do! Here's a challenge for you. If you ask me a riddle that I can't answer then I'll give you my tooth.
   That's fair isn't it? By the way, I think I know one of those boggarts— my little brother!
                              Love Holly